LOS TRES OSOS

PAUL GALDONE

Traducción de
Teresa Mlawer

Original title: The Three Bears
Text and illustrations copyright © 1972 by Paul Galdone
Book designed by Paul Galdone
Spanish translation copyright © 1996 by Lectorum Publications, Inc.
All rights reserved including the right of reproduction
in whole or in part in any form.
A Clarion Book. Published by special arrangement
with Houghton Mifflin Company
ISBN   1-880507-71-4 (PB)
        1-880507-23-4 (HC)
Printed in the U.S.A.

LECTORUM
PUBLICATIONS, INC.
111 EIGHTH AVE., NEW YORK, NY 10011-5201

Había una vez tres osos que vivían
en una casita en medio del bosque.

otro era
un oso de tamaño mediano,

Uno de ellos
era un oso pequeñito,

y el otro era
un oso grande.

Cada uno tenía su plato.

El oso pequeñito
tenía un plato pequeñito,

el oso mediano
tenía un plato mediano,

y el oso grande
tenía un plato grande.

Cada uno tenía su propia silla.

El oso pequeñito
tenía una silla pequeñita,

el oso mediano
tenía una silla mediana,

y el oso grande
tenía una silla grande.

Cada uno tenía su propia cama.

El oso pequeñito
tenía una cama pequeñita,

el oso mediano
tenía una cama mediana,

y el oso grande
tenía una cama grande.

Una mañana, los osos prepararon
una rica avena para el desayuno,
y la sirvieron en los platos.
Pero como estaba muy caliente,
decidieron dar un paseo por el
bosque hasta que se enfriara.

Mientras los tres osos paseaban,

llegó a la casa una niña
llamada Ricitos de Oro.

10

Primero, miró por la ventana,

luego, miró por el ojo de la cerradura.

Desde luego que no había nadie en casa.
Ricitos de Oro le dio vuelta al picaporte.

La puerta no estaba cerrada con llave
porque los tres osos eran muy confiados.
Como no le hacían daño a nadie, pensaban
que nadie les haría daño a ellos.

Ricitos de Oro empujó la puerta y entró.

La avena, todavía humeante,
estaba sobre la mesa.
¡Qué buen olor tenía!

Sin detenerse a pensar de quien era la avena,
Ricitos de Oro fue directamente a la mesa.

Primero, probó la avena
del plato grande,
pero estaba demasiado caliente.

Luego, probó la avena
del plato mediano,
pero estaba muy fría.

Finalmente, probó
la del plato pequeñito.

14

No estaba ni muy caliente, ni muy fría.
Estaba como a ella le gustaba,
y se la comió toda.

Entonces, Ricitos de Oro se dirigió a la sala
para ver qué otras cosas podía encontrar.

15

En la sala había tres sillas.

Primero, se sentó en la silla
del oso grande,
pero era muy dura.

Luego, se sentó en la silla
del oso mediano,
pero era demasiado blanda.

Finalmente, se sentó en la silla
del oso pequeñito.
No era ni muy dura, ni muy blanda.
Era la que le quedaba bien.
Se sintió tan a gusto que comenzó
a mecerse una y otra vez

hasta que…

la silla se rompió
¡y Ricitos de Oro cayó al suelo!

Entonces, Ricitos de Oro entró
al dormitorio de los tres osos.

Como tenía sueño,
se acostó en la cama grande,
pero la almohada era demasiado alta.

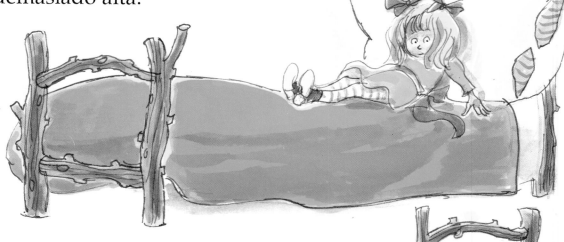

Entonces, se acostó
en la cama mediana,
pero los pies le quedaban muy altos.

Finalmente, se acostó
en la cama pequeñita.
Ni la cabeza le quedaba alta,
ni los pies tampoco.
Parecía hecha para ella.
Se sintió tan a gusto que se cubrió
con la colcha y se quedó dormida.

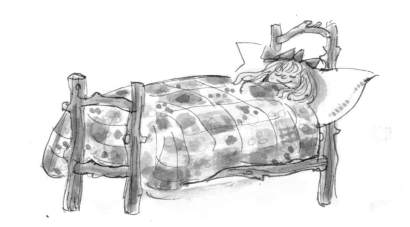

Al cabo de un rato,
los tres osos pensaron
que la avena ya estaría
lista para comerla.

Regresaron a casa
con mucho apetito.

Ricitos de Oro
había dejado la cuchara
dentro del plato del oso grande.
Tan pronto como él entró, se dio cuenta.

—¡ALGUIEN HA
PROBADO MI AVENA!
—dijo el oso grande,
con voz fuerte.

Ricitos de Oro también
había dejado la cuchara
dentro del plato del oso mediano.

—¡ALGUIEN HA PROBADO MI AVENA!
—dijo el oso mediano,
a media voz.

Entonces, el oso pequeñito fue a buscar su plato.

—¡ALGUIEN HA PROBADO MI AVENA
Y SE LA HA COMIDO TODA!
—dijo el osito,
con su vocecita.

Los tres osos se dirigieron
a la sala.

Ricitos de Oro había dejado
el cojín arrugado
en la silla del oso grande.
Tan pronto como él entró, lo vio.

—¡ALGUIEN SE HA
SENTADO EN MI SILLA!
—dijo el oso grande,
con voz fuerte.

23

Ricitos de Oro había dejado
el cojín aplastado
en la silla del oso mediano.

—¡ALGUIEN SE HA SENTADO EN MI SILLA!
—dijo el oso mediano,
a media voz.

24

En ese momento el osito vio su silla.

—¡ALGUIEN SE HA SENTADO EN MI SILLA
Y LA HA ROTO!
—dijo el osito,
con su vocecita.

Los tres osos entraron al dormitorio.

Ricitos de Oro había dejado la
almohada del oso grande fuera
de lugar. Tan pronto como
él entró, se dio cuenta.

—¡ALGUIEN SE HA ACOSTADO EN MI CAMA!
—dijo el oso grande, con voz fuerte.

Ricitos de Oro había levantado la
colcha de la cama del oso mediano.

—¡ALGUIEN SE HA ACOSTADO EN MI CAMA!
—dijo el oso mediano,
a media voz.

Entonces, el osito se acercó a su cama.

—¡ALGUIEN SE HA ACOSTADO EN MI CAMA
Y AQUÍ DUERME TODAVÍA!
—gritó el osito,
con su vocecita.

Al oír la voz del osito, Ricitos de Oro se despertó.

Cuando vio los tres osos a su lado,
se asustó tanto que dio una vuelta en la cama
¡y saltó por la ventana!

Corrió tan rápidamente como le permitieron sus piernas,
sin detenerse siquiera a mirar hacia atrás.

Nadie ha vuelto a saber de Ricitos de Oro.

Y los tres osos no la han vuelto a ver más.

Milk

Cereal

S P

What Happens to a

HAMBURGER?

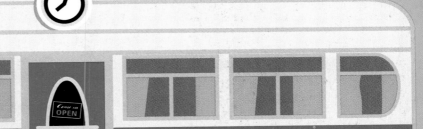

by Paul Showers · illustrated by Edward Miller

HarperCollinsPublishers

To my sister, Irene

—E. M.

Special thanks to Christine Frissora, assistant professor of medicine,
the Weill Medical College, Cornell University, for her expert advice.

The art in this book was created using the computer.

The *Let's-Read-and-Find-Out Science* book series was originated by Dr. Franklyn M. Branley, Astronomer Emeritus and former Chairman of the American Museum—Hayden Planetarium, and was formerly co-edited by him and Dr. Roma Gans, Professor Emeritus of Childhood Education, Teachers College, Columbia University. Text and illustrations for each of the books in the series are checked for accuracy by an expert in the relevant field. For more information about Let's-Read-and-Find-Out Science books, write to HarperCollins Children's Books, 1350 Avenue of the Americas, New York, NY 10019, or visit our website at www.letsreadandfindout.com.

HarperCollins®, ☀®, and Let's Read-and-Find-Out Science® are trademarks of HarperCollins Publishers Inc.

photo credits: p. 12 © Custom Medical Stock Photo; p. 14 © J. Siebert/Custom Medical Stock Photo; p. 17, p. 20 lower, p. 23 © Science Photo Library/Custom Medical Stock Photo; p. 20 upper © R. Becker/Custom Medical Stock Photo

Library of Congress Cataloging-in-Publication Data
Showers, Paul.
    What happens to a hamburger? / by Paul Showers ; illustrated by Edward Miller. — [Newly illustrated ed.]
        p.   cm. — (Let's-read-and-find-out science. Stage 2)
    Summary: Explains the processes by which a hamburger and other foods are used to make energy, strong bones, and solid muscles as they pass through the digestive system.
    ISBN 0-06-027947-8. — ISBN 0-06-027948-6 (lib. bdg.). — ISBN 0-06-445183-6 (pbk.)
    1. Digestion—Juvenile literature. [1. Digestion. 2. Digestive system.] I. Miller, Edward, ill.
II. Title. III. Series.
QP145.S49   2001
612.3—dc21
                                                                                    97-39007
                                                                                    CIP
                                                                                    AC

1 2 3 4 5 6 7 8 9 10 ❖ Newly Illustrated Edition

What Happens to a

HAMBURGER?

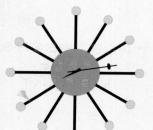

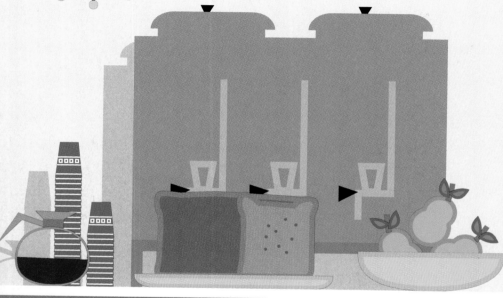

SANDWICHES

egg	peanut butter
steak	tuna fish
ham	turkey salad
BLT	bologna
cheese	pastrami

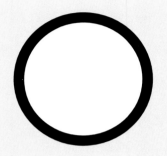

4

I like to eat.

I like bread and pears and celery. I like carrots and chicken and french fries and hamburgers. I like juice and milk.

What do you like?

Good food makes you strong and healthy. It gives you energy and helps you grow.

Your body uses food in different ways. It uses some kinds of food to make strong bones and hard teeth. It turns other food into solid muscles. It uses some of the food you eat to keep warm.

Before your body can do these things, it has to change the food. Solid foods like hamburgers and french fries have to be changed into liquids. Liquids like milk and juice have to be changed, too.

When you change the food you eat, you are digesting it.

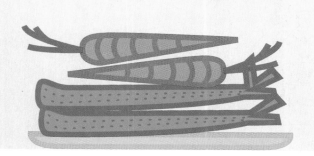

Put two cubes of sugar into an empty glass. Take a wooden spoon and pound the lumps with the handle. Pound them until they are broken up into powder.

Now pour some water into the glass and stir. Keep stirring until the sugar powder has disappeared.

Take a sip of the water. Can you taste the sugar? The sugar has disappeared, but it is still there. It has broken up into millions of tiny pieces. Your eye cannot see them, but your tongue can taste them.

Sugar
Cubes

When you digest your food, you break it up into millions of very tiny pieces. You start to do this as soon as you take a bite to eat. Digestion begins in your mouth when you chew. You break up the food with your teeth.

Get a piece of raw carrot and a plate. Take a bite of carrot and chew it ten times. Spit the carrot out onto one side of the plate. Take another bite. Chew it thirty times. Spit out that mouthful on the other side of the plate. Can you see the difference?

The longer you chew food, the smaller the pieces will be.

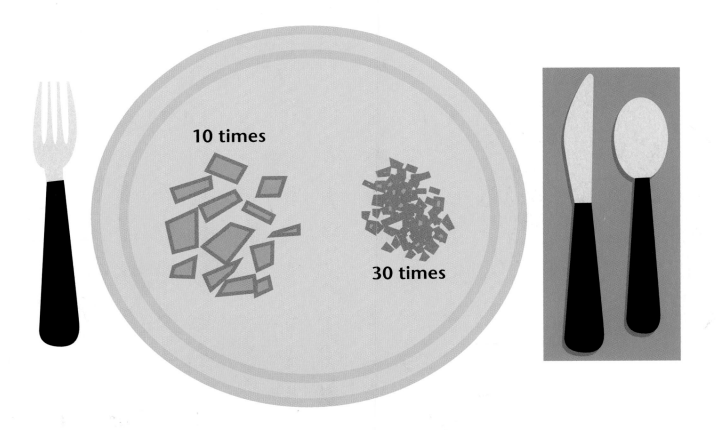

10 times

30 times

Something else helps to break up the food in your mouth. It is a fluid. Many people call it spit. Its scientific name is saliva.

Whenever you take a bite of food, saliva pours into your mouth. You say your mouth is watering. Saliva comes from small glands in your cheeks and under your tongue.

Sometimes saliva pours into your mouth even before you take a bite. The smell of food will start it. Take a good sniff of a brownie. Sniff an open jar of pickles. Now sniff a slice of pizza.

What other kinds of food make your mouth water?

Saliva

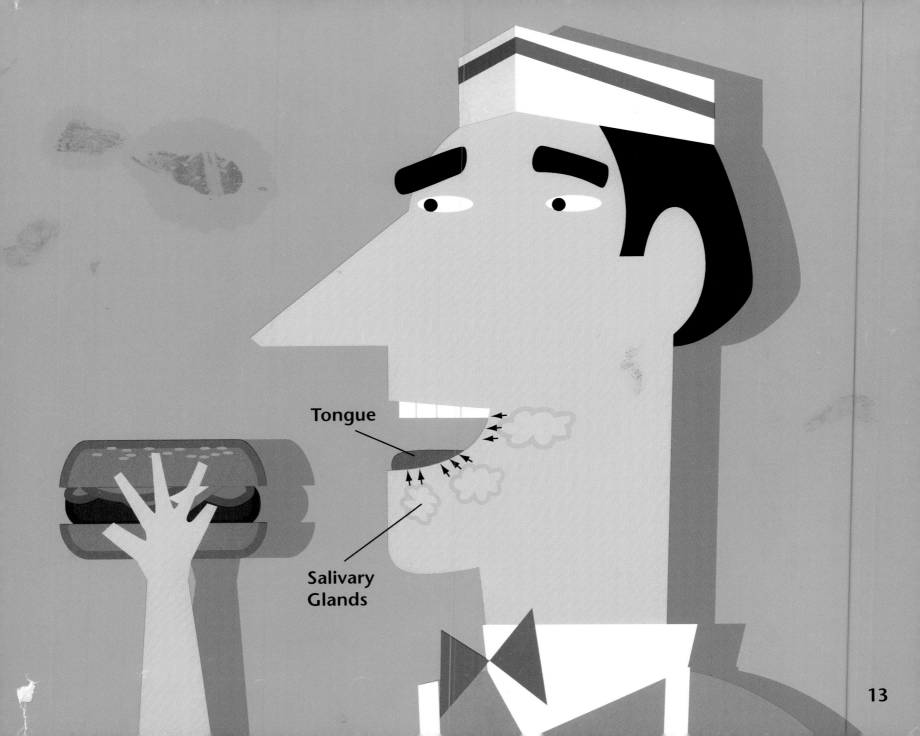

Tongue

Salivary
Glands

13

After you have chewed your food, you swallow it. Your epiglottis closes. That is a door that keeps food from going down your trachea (windpipe) and into your lungs. Your throat squeezes together when you swallow. It pushes food down into your esophagus. Another name for esophagus is gullet.

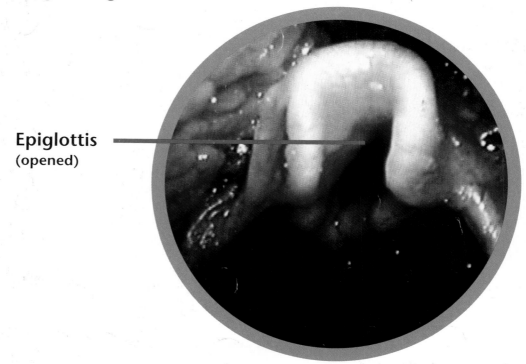

Epiglottis
(opened)

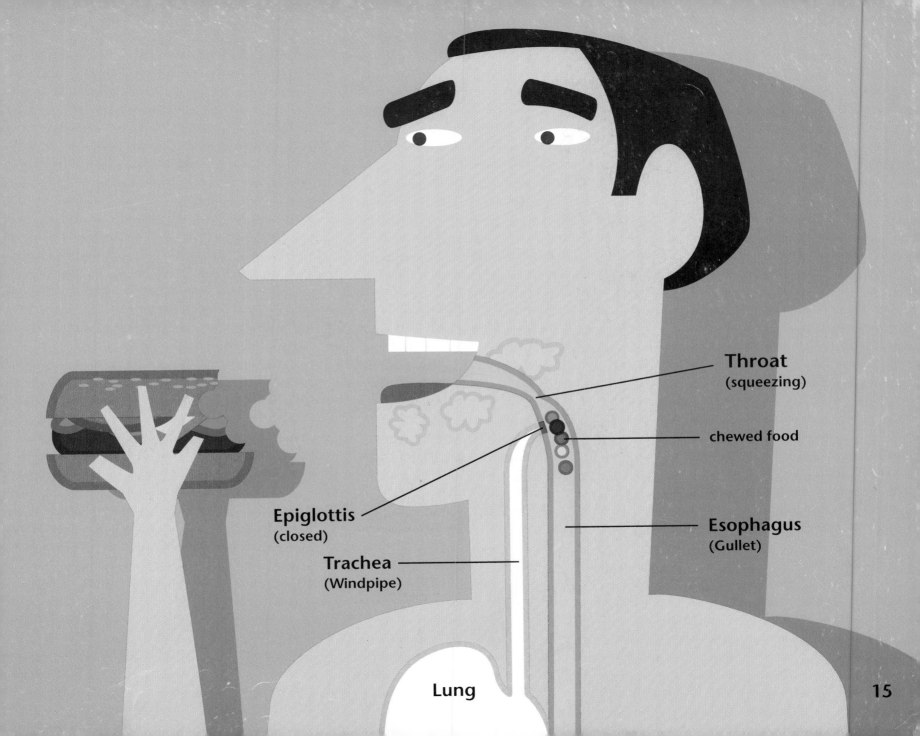

Throat
(squeezing)

chewed food

Epiglottis
(closed)

Esophagus
(Gullet)

Trachea
(Windpipe)

Lung

15

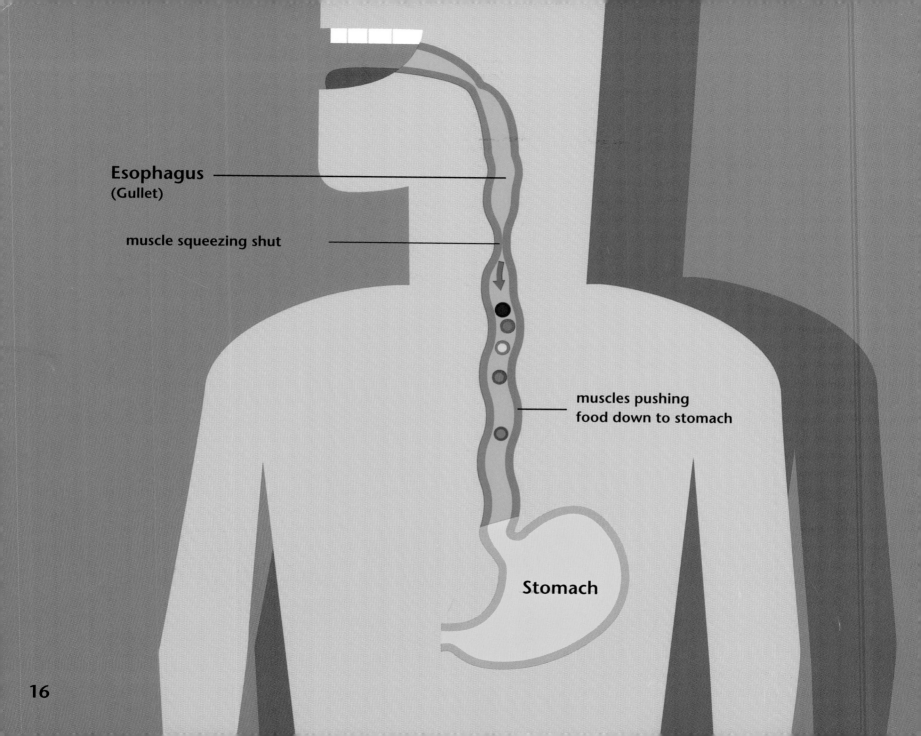

Esophagus
(Gullet)

muscle squeezing shut

muscles pushing
food down to stomach

Stomach

Your gullet is a tube that leads from the back of your mouth to your stomach. There are muscles in your gullet that squeeze together. They push food into your stomach.

Your stomach is a tube like your gullet. But there is a difference. Your stomach can stretch like a balloon. When you eat, your stomach stretches to hold the food.

Inside the Stomach

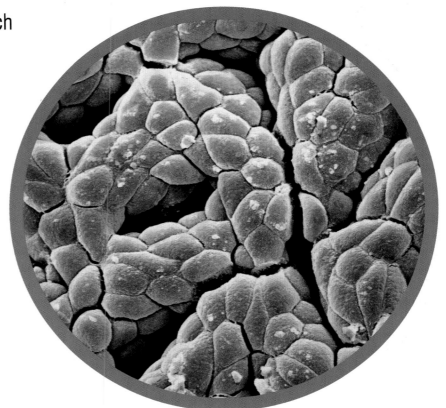

After you swallow your meal, your stomach muscles begin to squeeze. The food is mashed and stirred together.

Your stomach has fluids in it like the saliva in your mouth. They are called digestive fluids. They pour in from tiny glands in the sides of the stomach. The digestive fluids help to break the food up into smaller and smaller pieces.

Food stays in your stomach for several hours. Some kinds of food stay only about two hours. Other kinds stay longer. The food stays until all the lumps have been broken up. It is like a thick soup now. It is made of millions and millions of tiny pieces.

But digestion has just begun. The tiny pieces must be made even smaller. This happens in your intestines.

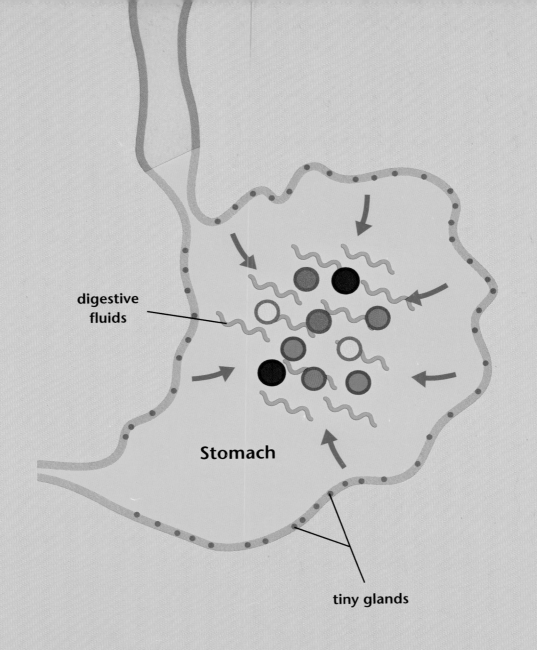

digestive fluids

Stomach

tiny glands

There are two intestines in your body—the small intestine and the large intestine. They are really one single, long tube. This tube is coiled up inside you like a pile of heavy rope. It is about twenty-one feet long.

Most of the tube is narrow and is called the small intestine. The last four or five feet of the tube are much wider. This part is called the large intestine.

Inside the Small Intestine

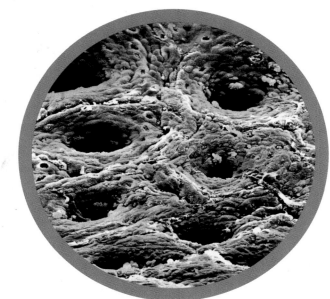

Inside the Large Intestine

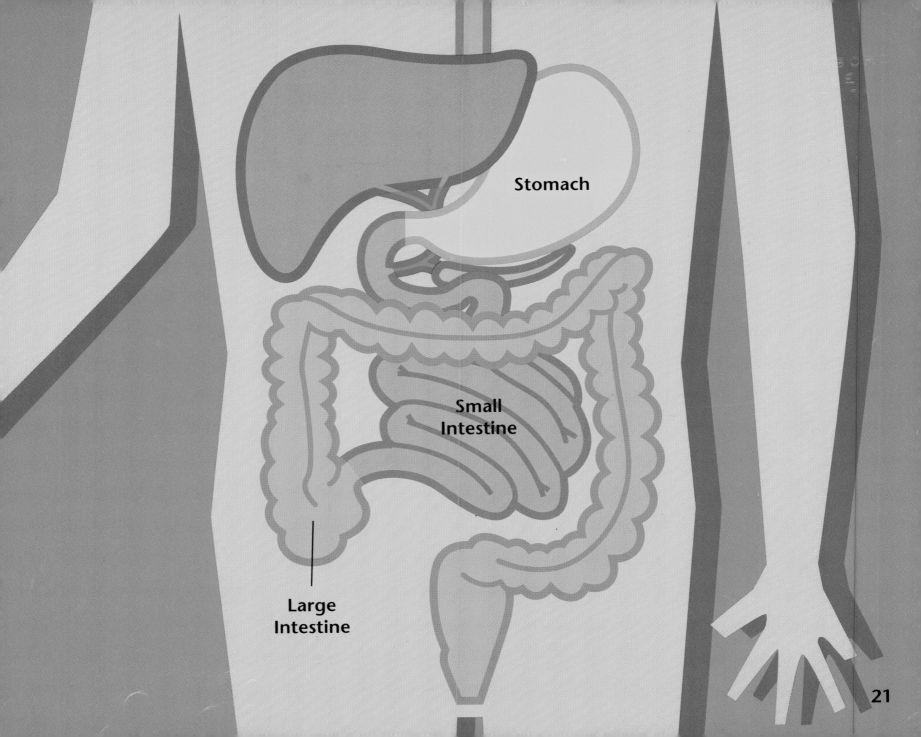

Stomach

Small
Intestine

Large
Intestine

21

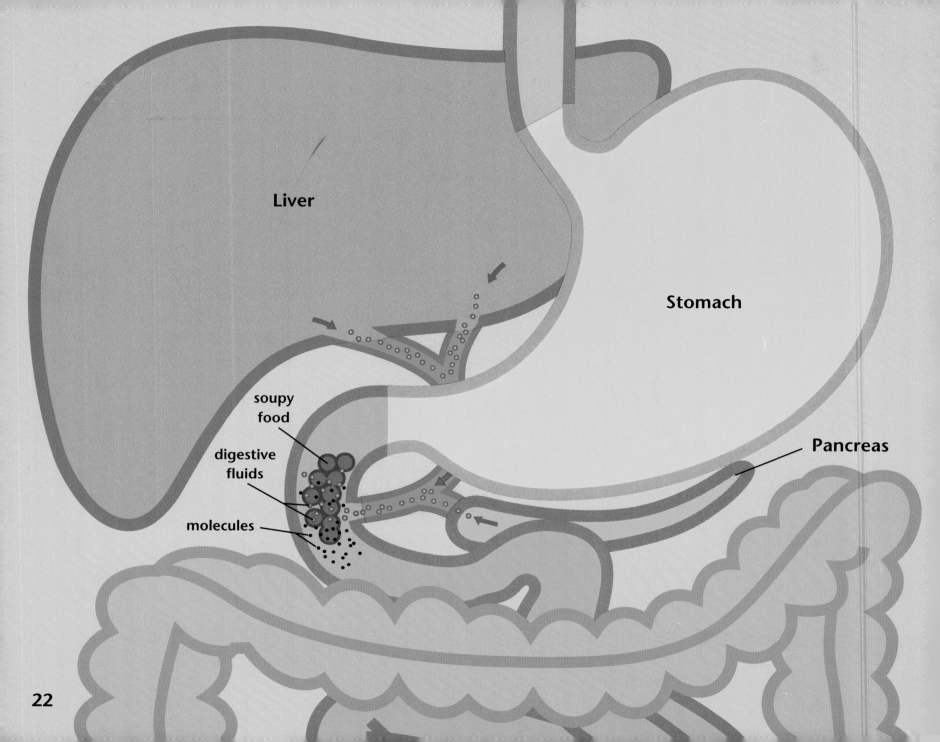

Liver

Stomach

Pancreas

soupy
food

digestive
fluids

molecules

22

The soupy food is squeezed into the small intestine from the stomach. Digestive fluids from the liver and another organ called the pancreas are mixed with the food in the small intestine. These fluids break the food up into very tiny pieces called molecules. Molecules are so small, you cannot see them without a special microscope.

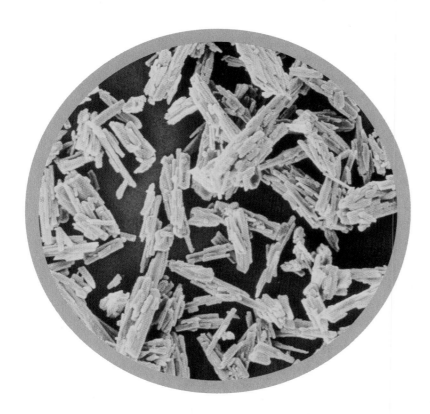

Groups of Cholesterol Molecules

The food molecules pass into tiny blood vessels and lymph vessels in the walls of the small intestine. They move into your blood. Then your blood carries them to every part of your body.

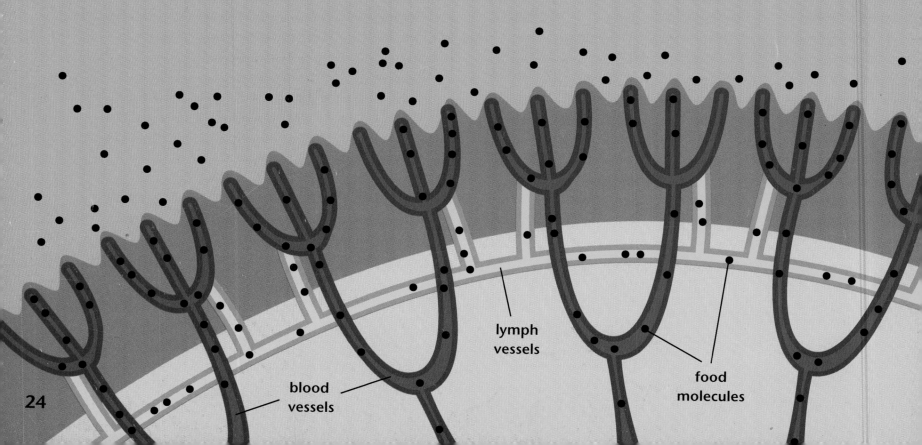

lymph
vessels

food
molecules

blood
vessels

24

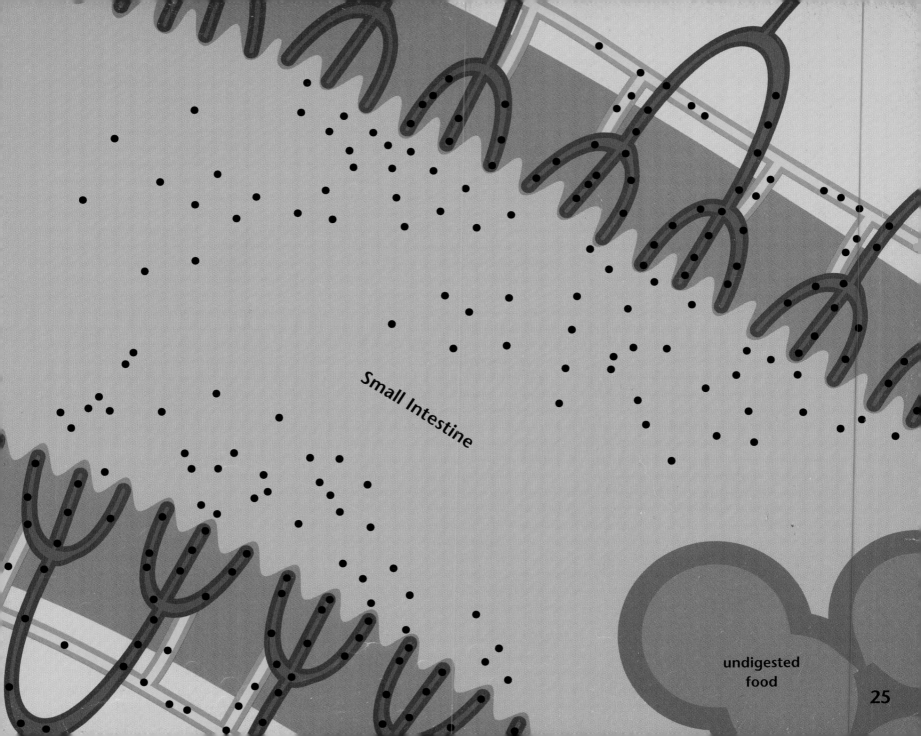

Small Intestine

undigested
food

25

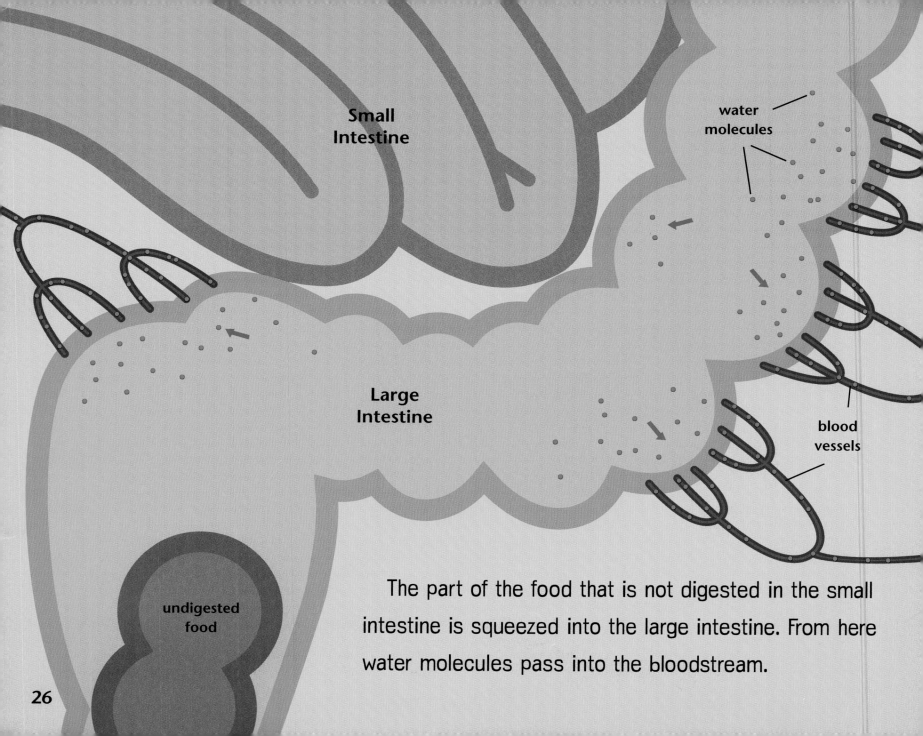

Small
Intestine

water
molecules

Large
Intestine

blood
vessels

undigested
food

The part of the food that is not digested in the small intestine is squeezed into the large intestine. From here water molecules pass into the bloodstream.

Your body cannot use all of the food you eat. The food it cannot use is stored in the large intestine. You get rid of the unused food when you go to the toilet.

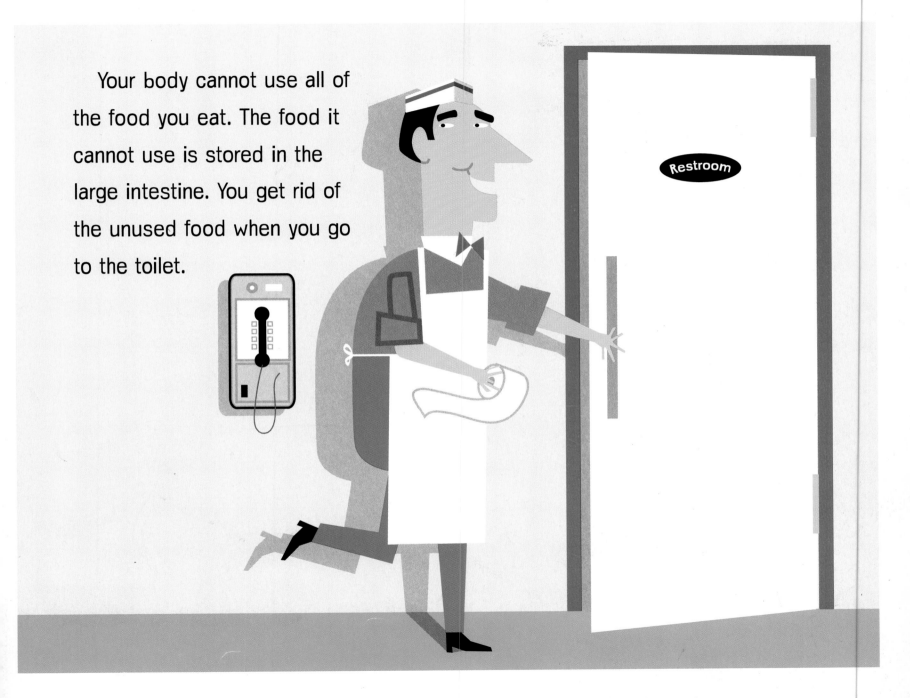

In the morning you may eat scrambled eggs or cereal. You may drink orange juice or milk.

In a few hours, your body has digested the food. Then your blood begins to carry the tiny food molecules—to your muscles to make them stronger...to your bones and teeth to make them harder...to every part of your body to give you energy and help you grow.

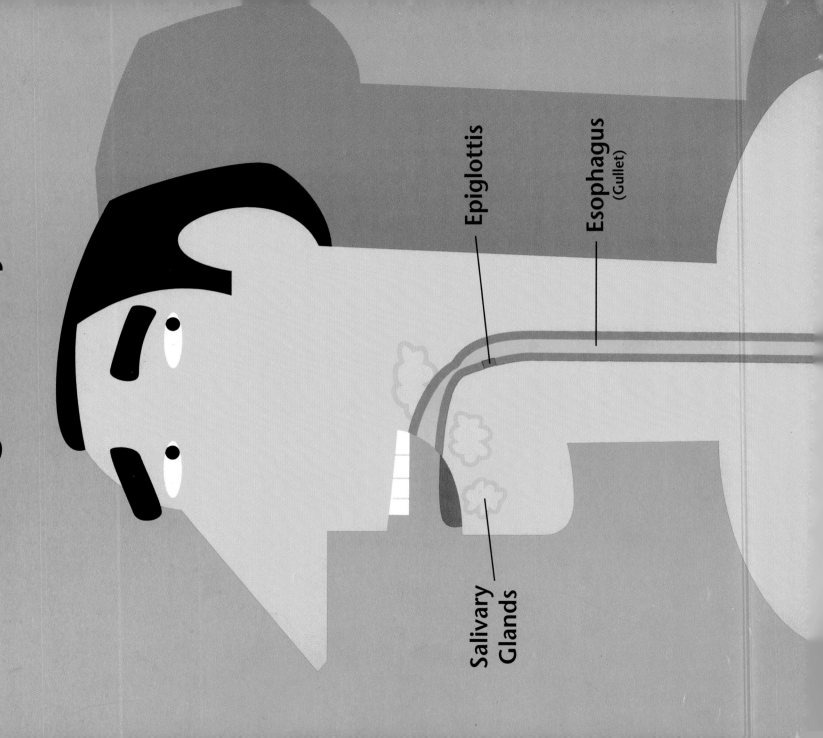

The Digestive System

Epiglottis

Esophagus
(Gullet)

Salivary
Glands

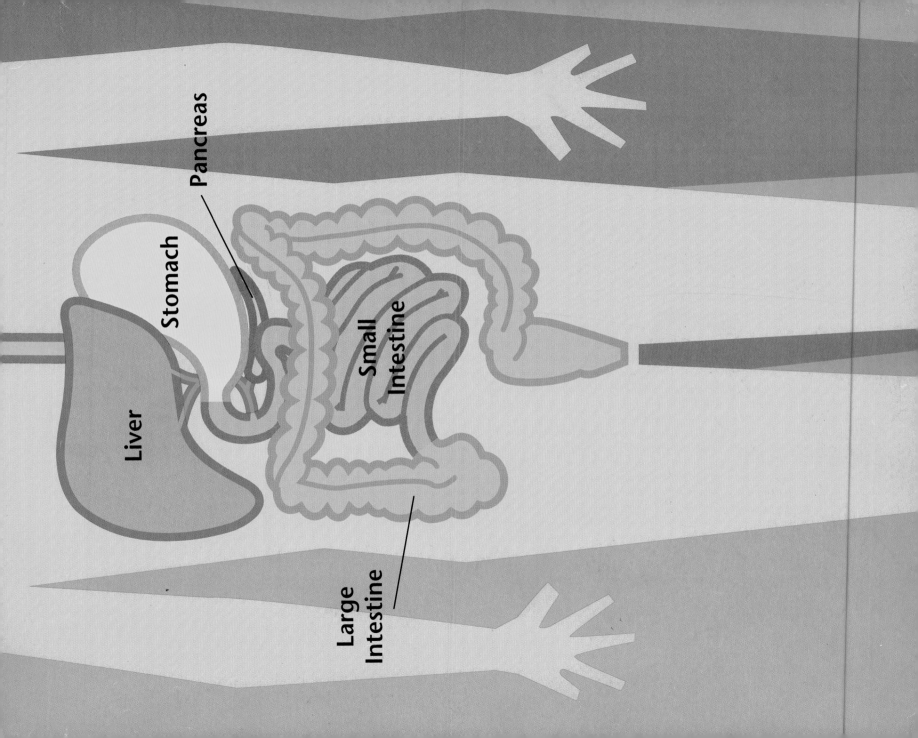

FIND OUT MORE ABOUT DIGESTION

How long is your small intestine?

1. Find a spool of string, a marker, and a pair of scissors.
2. Unroll the spool of string from the bottom of your foot to the top of your head.
3. Mark that spot on the string with a marker.
4. Place the part of the string with the spot under your foot, and unroll the spool until it reaches the top of your head again.
5. Repeat steps 3 and 4 one more time.
6. After you mark the third spot on the string, place that spot under your foot, and unroll the spool until it reaches your waist.
7. Mark that spot with the marker, and then snip the string with scissors at the fourth spot. The length of the string is about the length of your small intestine. It is about three and a half times as long as your own body is.

How do the digestive fluids in your body affect food?

Gather these materials:

2 clear-plastic cups	3 spoons	2 spoonfuls of lemon juice
a marker, pen, or pencil	6 spoonfuls of milk	plastic wrap
2 pieces of masking tape	2 spoonfuls of water	2 rubber bands

1. Label the cups "water" and "lemon" by writing the words on the two pieces of masking tape and then sticking one on the outside of each cup.
2. Put three spoonfuls of milk in each cup.
3. Use a clean spoon to add two spoonfuls of water to the cup labeled "water." Stir.
4. Use a clean spoon to add two spoonfuls of lemon juice to the cup labeled "lemon." Stir.
5. Cover each cup with plastic wrap. Use a rubber band to keep the plastic wrap in place.
6. Wait for about a minute and then look closely at each cup of milk. Write down what you see.
7. Wait two hours and then look closely at each cup of milk again. Write down what you see. You'll notice that the water doesn't change the milk. But the lemon juice separates the milk into a lumpy white mass at the bottom of the cup and a clear liquid at the top. Your stomach contains liquids that act on foods in the same way the lemon juice changes the milk.